The Whispering

The Whispering Earth: Book 1

Jana Harper

Published by Shady Beach Publishing – Asheville, North Carolina

The Whispering by Jana Harper

Copyright © 2012 by Shady Beach Publishing

Current edition Copyright © 2022 by Shady Beach Publishing

All Rights Reserved

The characters and events portrayed in this book are fictitious. Any similarity to real persons, living or dead, is coincidental and not intended by the author.

No part of this book may be reproduced, or stored in a retrieval system, or transmitted in any form or by any means, electronic, mechanical, photocopying, recording, or otherwise, without express written permission of the publisher.

ISBN-13: 9798474691152
ASIN: B094DKD7DV

Cover design made with Canva
Printed in the United States of America

THE WHISPERING

PROLOGUE

(This is an excerpt from the last few pages of a journal found buried in the ground.)

February 13, 1900

My name is Jacob Riley and I am 12 years old. I don't know how long I have left, but I hope that whoever finds this has better luck than I have had.

About a month ago we moved into this house…my parents wanted to celebrate the turn of the century, along with their new-found fortune with a new, much larger, house. When we first moved in I thought it seemed kind of spooky, but nothing too strange. It just gave me a kind of uneasy feeling when I first walked in. It wasn't until last week that things got weird.

I was exploring the yard when I chanced upon an old creek. I thought it seemed like a fun place to play around, so I stayed there for a while. I lost track of time and before I knew it the sun was setting. When I tried to find my way back, all I could find was trees, the house was no where in sight. As soon as the sun had fully set, I heard it. The whispers. They weren't coming from anywhere in the distance as you might expect, it was as if they were from my own head. It was the sound of hundreds of voices speaking quietly to one another, but I couldn't make out a single word of it. I couldn't take it any longer and my legs gave out, yet the whispers went on all night. The next morning my father found me passed out right behind the house.

The whole day I tried to forget about that night. I told myself that it had only been a dream, a horrible dream, a nightmare even. That evening I was in my room, waiting for the sun to set, praying that those horrible voices wouldn't start up again. I knew that it hadn't been a dream the night before; I knew they would be back that night. I was right. Once they started, I didn't know what to do, so I ran downstairs, startling my parents. They acted as if they didn't hear anything, they told me that it was just my imagination and sent me to bed. I knew I couldn't possibly imagine something as terrible as this.

The whispering has continued every night since then. The sun is starting to go down, now that I think of it.

February 19, 1900

I think things may be getting worse for us here. For one, the whispering has gotten slightly louder each night, it's become almost unbearable. Also, today while in town a man mentioned that there used to be a cemetery on our property, but the strange thing is that it was torn down shortly before we moved in. I wouldn't be concerned, but he said that the cemetery had been located beside a creek.

When we got back I decided to start searching for the creek again when I fell into a hole. It was very deep, about five or six feet down, but the creepy thing is that I was standing on a pile of bones. I don't understand what's going on here.

Why would I be hearing whispers at night just because of a cemetery in our yard? I want to see if I can find any more of those graves before it gets dark outside.

February 20, 1900

When I went out looking for those graves yesterday, I looked back into the one I fell into and saw that the bones were gone. Also, very early this morning, a strange old man was knocking at the door. He told us that we needed to leave this house or else bad things will happen to us. He said it in a really creepy voice and I think I might believe him. It was odd, his face seemed almost familiar to me, but I don't recall ever seeing him before. Anyway, he left immediately after delivering the message. After that we went into town and all of the people we asked said that they didn't know anyone by the description we had given them.

February 23, 1900

I think this might be my last journal entry. My parents are both missing. I'm afraid whatever happened to them will be happening to me. I have to hurry if I

(There was nothing in the journal after this, the rest of the pages are only smeared with blood.)

CHAPTER 1
July 20, 2000

I looked out of the car window as we finally pulled up to our new home. We had been looking forward to moving in for the past three months, and now we were finally here. My parents had been promising us a new house for the past two years, and since my dad got the new job they could finally afford it. It was an older house, built back in the 40s. There were three floors, and it was painted a darker shade of grey, but it was the yard that I was really looking forward to. The house came with sixty acres of land surrounding it, and I couldn't wait to start exploring.

The car engine cut off as my dad pulled the keys from the ignition. We all opened our doors and got out of the car. My legs wobbled a bit as they got used to standing once again. My younger brother, Josh, was the first to run up to the front door, leaving us behind to unpack the car. Tomorrow the rest of our things would be here as well.

*****

I had just finished unpacking my things when I walked out into the yard. I was determined to at least start exploring a bit before the end of the day. I decided to start by heading down a faint path. The yard was practically a forest; I could see no end to the trees.

I had been walking for just a short while when I saw a patch of dirt on the ground that seemed out of place. It looked as if someone had dug up something here and then filled it back in. I was curious as to what it might be. We didn't have anything with us at the moment to dig with, at least not until tomorrow. I got down on my knees and started clawing at the ground. It wasn't long until I discovered an old, worn book. It was falling apart at the seam and was still covered in dirt and mud.

The sun was starting to go down so I started walking back, still carrying the book in my hands. I opened the book to the middle as I walked. It was stained with what looked like blood and smelled incredibly old. The pages were extremely thin and many were torn. All of the words were handwritten. It looked like a journal or a diary. I heard a voice in the distance. Startled, I looked up before realizing that it was only my mother. She had been calling me down for dinner. I ran back to the house, and put the journal in my room before washing up for dinner.

*****

That night I was playing around with Josh when I decided to show him the journal in my room. I turned to the first page and read out loud, "My name is Jacob Riley."

My brother laughed, confused. "Riley?" He asked me, "But that's our name. Is this a joke?"

I was confused. He was right, Riley was our last name, but I had never heard of a Jacob Riley before. I looked at the date, "February 13, 1900."

No wonder, I hadn't heard of him, he wrote this a century ago. I smiled at my brother reassuringly. "Yeah, it's a joke," I told him. "It has to be," I said quietly to myself. I didn't want to freak out my 10-year-old brother.

Josh yawned, "I'm gonna go to my room now," and he walked out. He had a very short attention span. He was probably going in there to play with his toys or something, having already forgotten about the journal. I loved him for it though, we were very close.

I turned my attention back to the journal and continued reading it. It both fascinated and frightened me. I wasn't sure what to think of it. All of the things this Jacob Riley described in it made me wonder what had happened here a century ago. I wondered what could have become of him and his parents, and I was determined to find out.

CHAPTER 2
July 22, 2000

The rest of our things had arrived yesterday. Most of my things had been unpacked and my room now looked more like an actual room now. I was sitting at my desk looking at my computer monitor. I had decided to try looking up information on a Jacob Riley. The name came up to very few search results, none of them were about the Jacob Riley I was looking for. I groaned, I wasn't sure what I could search for that would give me any information on the subject. Then I thought, I could type in the town name instead.

When I typed in, "Monroe deaths in 1900," several articles finally came up. The first page of results was no use, but on the second page, I found a newspaper article that sounded quite interesting. "Strange deaths in local house," I clicked on the link and it took me to website that I had never heard of. This was strange; it said that the entire Riley family disappeared from their house on the same day. There was no trace of them found at all.

I went back to the search and scrolled down. There was another article, this time just about the house. It had been published in November of 1990. I clicked on the link. On the page there was a blown up picture of our house, and under that read, "Local house believed to be cursed." That was strange; you would think we would have heard something about that in the process of buying it. I continued reading, "This past May, the Holt family disappeared from their home without a trace, continuing the ongoing occurrence in this house. Every 10 years, since 1900, a family vanishes from the home without a trace, the majority of which have only resided there for a few weeks." The article went on in this manner for another two pages. I wasn't sure what to think of the article. If it was true, how could no one have mentioned it to us before we moved in?

While the article had freaked me out, I wanted to know more, so I continued reading it all the way through. It said that after another incident in 1940, the house had to be torn down, but a new one was constructed on top of it in 1947. That house must be the one we're living in now, I thought.

My parents were walking up the stairs, calling my brother and I to them. I quickly closed the article and turned off the computer monitor. I walked hurriedly out into the hallway to meet them. Josh was already here, I expect he ran out here to greet them. He loved the house and because of this had slightly more energy that usual. They were all smiling.

"We just wanted to see how you two were doing now that we're starting to settle in," My mother started, "How do you like it so far?"

"It's awesome, there's so much room here," Josh exclaimed excitedly.

My parents turned their heads to me, awaiting an answer. I nodded and said, "Yeah, it's great. Lot's of room." I was lying. After reading that article, this place scared me.

*****

That night, I was lying in bed, holding the journal in my lap. I had it open to the last page. I couldn't stop reading it, "My parents are both missing. I'm afraid whatever happened to them will be happening to me," I read it out loud in a hushed voice for the fifth time. I couldn't help but think that I would be facing this same situation sometime very soon. At least I didn't have to endure the sound of whispers at night, not yet at least. I wished that I could just put these uneasy feelings aside and just choose to believe that this house was a good thing for us. Why did I have to find this journal?

Right then, I decided that I wouldn't believe any of this to be true unless I was able to find the graveyard beside the creek. If that was real, then the rest of it had to be true. If not, then all of my fears could be laid aside. I shut the journal and tucked it under my pillow. I wouldn't be worrying about any more of this tonight. I closed my eyes and drifted off to sleep, pushing any negative thoughts away for the time being.

CHAPTER 3
July 23, 2000

I awoke with a start. I had been dreaming of a nightmare, my parents were both gone along with my brother, Josh. I was being chased by an old man whispering things that I couldn't understand. In the end he had caught up to me, and there was nothing more after that. It took me a moment to realize that I was awake, that it had only been a dream.

I climbed out of bed, staggering toward my closet, where I pulled out a pair of jeans and a t-shirt to wear. I felt as if I hadn't slept at all. My entire body was aching with pain. It took me several minutes to climb into my jeans and pull my shirt on, mostly because I tried to fall back to sleep after putting the jeans on.

    I walked downstairs, grabbed a pop tart off the counter, and poured myself a glass of milk before sitting down at the table. The room was empty, I assumed that Josh was already outside in the yard playing, and our parents were probably still in bed. After stuffing the food into my mouth I got up and walked out of the door. My brother was no where to be seen. He probably wandered off into the woods, I told myself, he'll be back.

    Now it was time for my search for the graveyard beside the creek to begin. I started into the woods, deciding to start in the place I had originally found the journal. It only took a few minutes to find the small hole in the ground. Loose dirt was still scattered around it, but there was something different about it. I crouched down beside it and looked down. What I saw made my heart almost stop beating. The hole had been filled, but not by dirt, but with blood. The blood was fresh too, it seemed. I wanted to scream for help but couldn't find my voice. When I opened my mouth, all that came out were strange croaking noises. I took a step back, away from the hole. My knees felt weak and I fell to the ground. I sat there for a moment, thinking.

This must be a sign. A sign from whoever doesn't want people living on this property. Whoever or whatever hasn't wanted anyone on the property for the past 100 years. No, I told myself, I couldn't believe all of that, this wasn't proof enough. I had to find the graveyard before any conclusions could be made. I stood back up and started walking again, leaving the bloody hole behind me.

After walking for several minutes I was ready to give up when I heard the sound of rushing water. I walked forward just a few more steps to uncover a creek, hidden this deep into the woods. I sighed. If the creek was real wouldn't the graveyard be real as well? There was no way I could find out, the graveyard had been torn down in 1900, there was no way that any of it could have survived this long. The creek was proof enough, wasn't it? No, it couldn't be true, I told myself, how could we move into a house that was cursed? It was ridiculous.

I turned back around to start heading back, but didn't get very far. With only my first step my foot had slipped into the ground a bit. I could only see down to my ankle. I pulled on my leg as hard as I could but only ended up falling headfirst to the ground, and I kept falling. My foot was freed as it was pulled from the ground by the force of my fall. The light around me had darkened, and my arm was hurting. I felt as if I was sitting on something, too. I sat up and tried to gather my senses.

I was in a hole in the ground, I realized. It was only about five feet deep and I could see the opening just above my head, but instead I looked back down. There were worms coming out of the sides of the walls, and from the ground. It also smelled really bad, I could hardly take it. I tried to move my arm. It worked, but hurt a lot. It looked like I had gotten a large bruise on it. I sat up on my knees to examine what had been poking my thigh this whole time. That was when I saw it. I held back a scream as I saw that there was a finger there, well, the bones of a finger. In fact there were bones strewn everywhere in this hole. Where was I? Then I remembered. I was sitting in one of the graves from the old graveyard. How had it survived this long, I wondered.

I stood up, my head barely outside of the hole. It took only a moment to climb out. I walked back home solemnly, wishing I had never found the graveyard, wishing that we had never moved into this house. By the time I walked back in, my mom was making lunch. She smiled at me once she saw me and asked how my morning had been.

"It was okay," I lied once again, "I was just exploring the yard again."

My mother nodded and returned back to what she had been doing. I walked back up to my room and read through the journal again, wondering if the events described in it would be happening to us anytime soon.

CHAPTER 4
July 23, 2000

I was lying back in bed after dinner. The journal was there beside me, opened to the middle, where the words ended and the blood trails began. I could see the trees through the window across from my bed. The sun was setting, and the sky was pink. My mind was racing. I was afraid. I didn't want to disappear like this Jacob Riley and his family had 100 years ago. I couldn't get my mind on anything else; I was too worried, too afraid. All I could do was watch the sun as it slipped down into the earth.

That was when I heard it. The moment the sky went dark, I heard a voice. Not just one, dozens, and then what sounded like hundreds. They were all whispering. Some sounded as if they were arguing, others sounded as if they were chanting, but I couldn't completely make out what any of them were saying. I couldn't tell where they were coming from. I covered my head with my pillow, but they still spoke. I put in some ear phones and started playing music, but the voices drowned out all of it. It was just like Jacob had said. These voices were coming from my own head, but why?

I had to stop them. I couldn't listen to it all night; I would go crazy before the sun rose again. I started yelling with them, determined to be louder than them. It wasn't anything particular that I was saying, just gibberish. I would do anything to just make them shut up. My parents rushed into the room and asked what was wrong. Their voices took my focus away from the whispers for a brief moment. I tried answering them but couldn't find the words to say it. My parents looked concerned and were speaking to me but I couldn't tell what they were saying. I could see their lips move, but all that I could hear were the whispers. I couldn't take it anymore, and I started to feel weak. My eyes started to close and my limbs went limp. I fell back to my bed and felt more at peace than I had in the past few minutes. That was when I lost consciousness.

*****

I awoke on the couch the next day. My mom was sitting beside me. She smiled once she saw my eyes open, and my father walked in. He was holding a cup of coffee which he handed to me. I sat up and took a sip as my dad sat in the chair across from me.

"How are you feeling," my mom started after a moment of silence.

"Fine," I answered, trying to give a convincing smile.

"Do you know what happened last night?" My dad asked.

"I just freaked out I guess," I didn't want to freak out my parents by telling them what was going on. They probably wouldn't believe me anyway.

My dad raised an eyebrow questioningly, then said, "I guess we should call the doctor and tell him not to come then, but it's probably too late now."

"Doctor?" I asked, I didn't want to see a doctor, I hated doctors.

"We were very worried about you after what happened last night," my mother answered.

There was a knock at the door. We all jumped in surprise. "He came fast," my dad stated as he walked over to the door and opened it. The man at the door didn't look like a doctor at all. He was an older gentleman wearing very shabby looking clothes. I couldn't quite put my finger on it but he looked like someone I knew. Maybe a teacher from school, or I had seen him in town once, I didn't know. Then I remembered the journal. Jacob had mentioned a familiar looking older man in it. He had appeared shortly before him and his family had disappeared. I stood up and walked up beside my dad to face the man myself.

The man looked down at me. I didn't know what it was, he didn't look like he was doing anything, but I felt like he saw me. Not just physically, but like he saw that I was afraid of him and what he meant to us. He saw that I had read the journal, but I didn't know how he could. The man returned his gaze to my father.

"I am afraid I'll have to ask you and your family to leave this house," the man said in an unnaturally deep voice. It was strange and sounded almost unearthly. "You will have to leave immediately or things of a horrible nature will happen to you all. Good day." With that the man just walked away, leaving my parents looking quite puzzled. I, on the other hand, imagine that I looked quite terrified.

CHAPTER 5
July 24, 2000

We just stood there for a moment, trying to process what the man had said and why he had said it. Well, I'm sure that's what my parents were doing. I knew exactly what he had been saying, but I still didn't know why any of this was happening. Why us, I wondered. My dad was the first one to move.

He turned around to my mother and asked, "What was that man going on about? Must be crazy," and with that he just walked off, seeming to forget everything we had spoken of before the encounter. My mother on the other hand still looked dazed as she was still trying to process everything. It had to be confusing for them, with me having the ordeal with the whispers, and now a crazy old man telling us that we had to leave the house or bad things would happen. The journal was both a blessing and a curse in this way I suppose. It was true, ignorance is bliss. I'm sure neither of my parents felt the amount of fear in them that I am feeling now.

    I walked out of the room and back up the stairs. My dad was sitting in his chair at his writing desk. He was on the phone.

    "Yes, an old man," my dad was saying, "I would say he was at least in his late seventies, if not older."

He sat there, listening for a moment before continuing, "No, I don't know him. He just came by our house and told us to leave. I believe he was threatening us as well."

He listened again, "No, I wouldn't take it too seriously, but I don't appreciate what he did at all. He frightened my wife and son half to death I believe. Yes…yes, thank you, if you could look into it, yes, okay, thanks. Okay, bye then." He put the phone back down and looked over to me, giving a half-smile. "I was just reporting that man to the police," he explained, "He did threaten us after all."

I only nodded before I continued on to my room. Upon entering, I looked over to my bed, where the journal lay in the center. I walked over and picked it up. Looking again to the final pages. I flipped back a page and read Jacob's description of the old man again. It wasn't too detailed but it sounded like the man I had just encountered. How could something like this happen to us? We only wanted a decent home to live in, not some haunted house that would be the end of all of us. I closed my eyes and tried to think of our lives before we moved here.

*****

I awoke just as the sun started to sink down to the ground again. I sat up. How had my parents let me sleep this long? I had to have missed lunch and dinner by now; they would never let me sleep through that. I walked out of my room and looked around. The hall was empty. I opened the door to my brother's room to check. He was sitting on the floor playing with a toy. I gave a sigh of relief before jogging down the stairs to see my parents sitting at the table together. They looked up at me and smiled.

"You were tired," my mother said, "You slept through lunch and dinner. Why don't you go ahead and fix yourself something to eat."

I grabbed a snack from the pantry and ate it quickly before running back upstairs. I was glad to see that my family was still here, I had thought for sure that they had disappeared like Jacob's had. Right now I had to hurry back to my room before the whispers started again. It would be a long night.

*****

I awoke the next morning later than usual. It was almost noon. Last night had been rough. The whispers had come as soon as I had gotten back to my room. At first I had wanted to scream, but I didn't want to startle my family again, instead, I put in some earphones and tried my best to focus on the music rather than the voices. It didn't work very well, but all the effort tired me out and I had fallen asleep around two-thirty in the morning, exhausted. I was just glad it was over, but I knew I would have to go through it again tonight, and tomorrow night, and the night after that. For now, I was just happy that I had some peace and quiet.

I got dressed and walked downstairs. My dad was sitting at the table with my brother eating soup. My mom walked in from the kitchen and took her seat next to Dad as I jumped from the last step. There was an extra bowl of soup already in my spot at the table. I sat down and started to eat it.

"I'm glad you were able to join us in time for lunch today," my dad said in a slightly sarcastic voice. My mother smiled slightly at this comment.

We sat in silence for a few moments as we ate. Then I thought of the family that had lived here in 1900 and asked, "Did you know that there were Riley's that lived here before us?"

My dad looked at me questioningly, "Really? Well, not any that are related to us, I wouldn't expect."

"Well, it was a long time ago. In 1900 actually," I continued.

My parents both stared at me blankly for a second. "Where did you hear about this," my dad asked.

"Oh, someone mentioned it when we were in town once," I lied quickly.

"Well, this house was built in the 1940s, so that would be impossible anyway," my dad said matter-of-factly.

"Actually, this house was built on top of the property of an older house, the one that they lived in," I blurted out without thinking.

"And you heard about this in town as well," my father questioned.

"No," I answered quickly, "I read it on the internet."

"Really, and what were you looking our house up for on the internet?"

"I just wanted to know the history of the place, that's all."

The rest of the meal was finished in silence.

CHAPTER 6
July 25, 2000

That afternoon, we went into town. My dad wanted to check-in at the police department to see if they had found the old man yet. When we arrived the town was busy. At least for its size. The entirety of the town, Monroe, consisted of three roads that intersected each other in the middle. All of the buildings on these roads were only two or three floors tall. It was a nice, old-timey town that wasn't overly crowded. The people seemed decently mannered as well.

When we got to the police department my dad walked in, leaving my mom, Josh, and myself to wait in the car. He kept on saying that the incident yesterday with the old man wasn't that big of a deal, but he wasn't acting like it. I was glad that he was taking such measures though. While it may not be of any help at all, anything that may stop our impending doom would be a blessing upon us, whether he knew it or not. I knew that it probably wouldn't help and that we would probably start disappearing soon, but any hope, false or not, was more than welcome to me.

My father was walking back to the car a moment later. He sat down in the car and slammed his door shut, then looked over to our mother.

"They said that they haven't been able to find anyone that matched the description," he explained, "This is a small town; it shouldn't be that hard to find a crazy old man who's been running around threatening people to get out of their houses."

"I'm sure they'll find him eventually," my mom said reassuringly.

My father sighed, before turning back to the wheel and starting the car. We stopped by the grocery store so that my mom could pick up a few things before we headed home. When we got back, I went up to my bedroom and sat at my computer desk.

I wanted to know more about the Riley family that lived here before us. I turned on my desktop and opened up the internet. I typed in, "Riley family, Monroe 1900." It said that there were over 200 results but only the top three had any seemingly relevant information in them. I clicked on the link to the first one, which took me to an older website. The article was short, only one paragraph. All it said was that the family had strangely disappeared in 1900, but there was an old picture with it. It showed the family standing in front of the house, all smiling except for the father. I clicked back, and went to the second website. This one was a little longer but didn't have any new information in it. The same picture was show at the top of the page. I sighed and went to the third page.

The article on the third page consisted of five paragraphs and a photo of the house without the Riley family in front of it. Strangely the article was titled "Riley Family: Vanished or Murdered?" This was something I hadn't seen before in my research on the family. I glanced at the publication date; the article was published in a local newspaper in 1971. I began reading the article, "The Riley Family vanished from their home 71 years ago. This occurrence has continued every decade as new families buy the home, which was rebuilt in 1947 after it was demolished in 1940, only to disappear shortly after, often within a matter of weeks. It has been observed that a common theme in each of these disappearances is a threat made by an older man. Most of the victims reported an older man showing up at the door and telling them to leave or 'bad things will happen.' The man has never been identified, and is undoubtedly a different man for each decade, leading us to suspect a link between the disappearances and the mysterious cult The Blood of the Earth, whose existence has never been confirmed. The cult has been known for kidnapping and murder, but they have never been caught due to the fact that no member has ever been discovered. It is believed that the cult may have kidnapped the Riley family and all subsequent victims and hidden their bodies. No evidence has been found to support this claim, however."

It sounded like a more extreme theory, but anything was possible with all of this. What were the odds that we would move in to a cursed house anyway? My mother yelled up the stairs for us to come down for dinner.

CHAPTER 7
July 25, 2000

After dinner we were treated to a surprise visit by my uncle, our only relative in the area. Now that I thought of it, he was probably the one that recommended this house to my parents. My Uncle Ray had always been close to our family, but before now it had always been hard to see him often since we had previously lived in different parts of the state. My brother Josh and I walked into the living room to greet him. Our parents were sitting on the couch with him when we walked in, chatting about the house. Uncle Ray smiled when he saw my brother and I walking toward him. My brother ran ahead of me to hug Uncle Ray. I, on the other hand, just stood behind him smiling.

"Hey boys," Uncle Ray exclaimed, "How are you two settling into your new home?"

"Oh, its awesome Uncle Ray," Josh shouted excitedly, "I have my own room here you know?"

Uncle Ray turned to me, awaiting my reply. I nodded, "Its good. I like it."

He smiled, "I knew you all would love it. You know, I don't think anyone's lived here for a couple of years. It's a shame. It's so beautiful here. I would've bought the house myself if I had the money, but I'm glad it went to you," Uncle Ray turned back to my parents, "Now we'll be able to see each other all the time, just like old times."

My parents laughed, and my dad stood up. "Could I get you a drink," he asked my uncle casually.

"Oh, I wouldn't want to bother you with it," Uncle Ray said. "You just moved in."

"Come on," my father insisted.

"All right then," Uncle Ray gave in, "but not too much."

My dad nodded and walked hurriedly into the kitchen. It was at this time that my uncle turned back to me with a questioning look on his face. "And what have you been up to lately?" he asked, "I mean, other than moving into a new house." He laughed a bit after he said this. I just looked at him with a blank face.

"You know," I answered, "the usual. Play around with Josh, sit on the computer for a while, oh and I've also spent a bit of time exploring the yard." I made sure to leave out the part where I found the bloody journal buried in the ground. Uncle Ray smiled at my answer.

"It's quite a big yard isn't it," he said. "Lot's of room for two growing boys. Just make sure you don't get lost out there after dark. This house has a lot of land surrounding it, so it's easy to wander too far."

The last part of his answer freaked me out a bit. What did he mean for us not to get lost after dark? Did he know something about the journal or the whispers or was he just saying it because he was concerned for us? My dad walked back into the room trying to balance the glasses of wine in his hands. Uncle Ray stood up and took one of them from him with a smile. My dad handed the other to my mom before he sat back down. We sat in silence for a few seconds as they all sipped their wine.

"So," my dad said, trying not to sound too awkward, "what have you been up to Ray?"

Uncle Ray grinned as he answered, "Well, I've been working down at the police station for a couple months now."

My dad looked surprised, "Oh, really? What happened to that bookshop of yours?"

"I just couldn't afford it," he answered solemnly. "It wasn't getting enough business to last, so I closed it down back in March and started working at the police station."

My brother, Josh, yawned. He was obviously bored with the conversation and walked out of the room and back up the stairs. My parents didn't seem to notice.

"Well, that's too bad about the business," my dad answered, "but I'm glad you found something else to do with your time. They give you a lot of work down there? I wouldn't guess this town was that big on crime?"

"Oh, you'd be surprised," Uncle Ray said.

"Really," my dad said questioningly.

"Don't get me wrong. It's a great town," Uncle Ray said quickly, "very peaceful to live in, but every town has some of those people who just can't seem to help themselves. Of course, we don't get anything big that often."

The Whispering

I glanced out of the window, seeing that the sun was going down. I knew I couldn't stay down here after dark, not with the whispers going on in my head. No one seemed to notice my exit either, as I stepped away from the living room and ran upstairs to my bedroom. I knew I probably wouldn't be getting any sleep tonight, just as I hadn't in the past couple nights, but I figured it was best to at least try. I slipped into my bed and closed my eyes as the whispers began to enter my mind.

CHAPTER 8
July 26, 2000

The next morning, I woke up feeling more tired than I had when I had first got to bed. I looked at the clock and gasped. It was 1:30 PM. I had never slept that long before in my life. How had my parents allowed me to sleep so long? I jumped out of bed, and sprinted down the stairs. It was empty, I couldn't hear a sound. Turning around, I ran back up the stairs and checked my brother's room. He wasn't there. I checked my parent's room. Empty.

I ran up to the third floor, my heart pounding. There wasn't a single person in the entire house.

I ran over to the window and peaked out. The car was still in the drive way, so I told myself they didn't go into town. The only place left to check was the backyard which wasn't likely for my parents. I quickly walked back down the stairs and bolted out through the back door. There was no one in sight, but the property was so large that they could be anywhere. I started for the creek where the old graveyard was. I knew that they wouldn't be there, but I had to check. When I arrived, breathless, I looked in all directions. There was no one here. I kept an eye out for any open graves, in case I fell in again. Perhaps my parents had taken Josh for a walk through the woods, I thought. But they weren't. I knew they were gone. They had all disappeared just like the Riley's that lived here before us and all the others in between.

How could they have just disappeared? Had they been kidnapped? I didn't know. All I knew was that I was alone now. I walked back to the house wondering what to do. Maybe if I could ask around town, someone would know something. But how would I get there? I couldn't drive. Besides, my parents had the keys to the car, and they were gone. It would be hard, but I could walk there, I thought. The house wasn't that far away from town; it wouldn't take too long to get there. Yes, I could walk there and get back before the sun went down. It was the best plan I had, so far.

I grabbed my wallet, which only had a few dollars in it, and I walked out of the house again. Our house came off of the main road to town, but it had a very long drive way, about a mile long actually. This was because the land was evenly distributed on all four sides of the house. I took a deep breath and started walking.

The drive way was a long, yet narrow, dirt road surrounded by old trees. I heard a snap and froze. I was breathing exceptionally hard, and I glanced behind me, looking for the source of the sound. There was nothing. It must have been a squirrel. I tried to reassure myself. I continued on, only to hear another snap a second later. This time it had been much louder. It almost sounded like a branch rather than a twig. I didn't want to take any chances and started running for the main road. It didn't take long to get there at this new, much faster pace. I came to an open road within five minutes.

Breathless and tired, my body wanted me to rest, but I knew that I shouldn't.

I glanced back down the dirt road looking for any potential pursuers. There was nothing in sight. As I began to turn my head back, I caught a glimpse of something dark shifting about in the corner of my eye. My head whipped back to face the dirt road once again, my eyes scanning it. There was nothing. Whatever I had seen, or thought I had seen, was no longer there. I realized that I had not breathed, and I took a deep breath before starting down the main road. I glanced back one last time, just to check. This time I saw something moving in the distance.

CHAPTER 9
July 26, 2000

My heart started pounding in my chest and I began to walk faster. I didn't know what it was but it was moving in my direction. I thought that it might be safer on the other side of the road. I looked, checking for any traffic. There was none, so I ran across as quickly as I could and continued on, looking over my shoulder from time to time. Whatever it was, it seemed to disappear at some point during all of this, but I didn't want to seem careless.

It took me about half an hour to make it to town. I hadn't seen anything following me since then either. I hadn't planned on what I would do once I reached the town, so I decided to start by asking around on the street. The first person I saw was a middle-aged man waiting at the bus stop alone, I walked up to him. He seemed confused at first, but I asked if he had heard anything strange about our house and he shook his head.

"Oh yeah," he said, "they say that house is cursed, someone disappears in it every ten years. Haven't heard anything this year though. Not yet at least."

"Do you know who lives there now?" I guessed he didn't since he didn't recognize me but I thought I could ask anyway.

"No, there was a nice young couple living there a couple years ago, but they left pretty quickly after they heard all of the rumors about it," he answered quickly. "Why do you ask?"

This man didn't know anything about my family's disappearance, so I decided it would be best to move on. Then I remembered one thing. It could be worth asking about. "Do you know anything about a cult by the name of 'The Blood of the Earth?'"

The man gave me a suspicious look. "No, now I would appreciate it if you left me alone now."

He was lying. I could tell, but I decided that it would be best for me to move on to someone else anyway. "Well, thank you for your time," I said before walking farther down the sidewalk.

The town wasn't busy at all right now; in fact there were barely any people on the streets. It was burning up outside. I looked up at the sign for the store ahead of me, McCaulkins Used Books. Maybe someone would be in there, I thought to myself.

I walked into the store and looked around. There was no one in the building besides the clerk at the desk, whose face was in a book and didn't seem to notice me as I walked in. She was a younger woman, probably in her early twenties, with long red hair. I walked up to the desk counter clearing my throat, hoping for her to notice. She looked up and smiled after realizing that I could be a potential customer.

"Can I help you?" she asked in a sweet voice.

"Yes, actually," I answered. "I was wondering if you had any material in here about a house people say is cursed around here."

"Um, not that I know of, but I can check," she answered, still smiling as she turned to her computer. "We have our entire catalogue listed here, so it'll just take a second."

"Okay, thanks," I smiled back and waited as she typed something in on the keyboard.

She turned back to me after only a short time, "No, I'm afraid we don't have anything on that. If you're looking for information on it you could probably just ask around town a bit. That or look it up on the internet. Do you need help with anything else?"

I thought for a moment before answering, "Yes, um, I was also wondering if you happened to have anything about the cult called 'The Blood of the Earth' by any chance."

She stopped smiling. "No, you won't find anything about them anywhere, because they don't exist," she answered in a raised voice.

I wasn't sure why no one seemed to want to talk about this cult. It was as if it was some sort of taboo subject around here. I tried to smile back at her as I slowly backed away towards the door. "Well, thanks anyway for your time, I'll go now."

I opened the door and walked out at a quickened pace. As I was closing the door, I saw something reflecting on the glass. It was like a dark shadow in the distance, right at the end of the tree line, in the direction I had come from. It was too far away for me to make out exactly what it was; and when I turned around to look, it had vanished. Now, it was really starting to scare me. It was as if this thing was following me, but I didn't know what it was. What if it was the same thing that took away my parents and brother? I was determined that it wasn't going to take me.

I started walking towards the police station. I had to tell someone that my family was missing. As I got closer, I started to think, "What if they won't let me leave since I am under eighteen and my parents are gone?" I had to go find out what it was that took them. Maybe going to the police wasn't such a good idea. I had to make up my mind quickly because I could see the station ahead of me.

I took a deep breath and turned back around. I couldn't risk it, I told myself. I had to find whatever had taken them on my own. The police wouldn't believe me anyway. They would probably think I was crazy and not even investigate it at all. I thought of my Uncle Ray, but even if he were to help, it would take them too long. I had to start looking for them by myself, and what better place to start than back at the house. I sighed as I realized that I would have to walk all the way back alone. My stomach growled. I hadn't eaten all day. I should at least stop for something to eat before going back.

CHAPTER 10
July 26, 2000

I was walking back down the sidewalk in the direction of my house. This trip hadn't been as successful as I had hoped it would be. Well, I would just have to make up for it by doing a bit more research on this cult when I got home. And then what, I wondered. I would just have to take this one step at a time. I was just so tired. I had barely slept at all since I found the journal. This whole move had turned into a huge nightmare for all of us.

Just as I turned to walk into the drive way, I saw something moving towards me again out of the corner of my eye. It wasn't moving very fast and it was still too far away to recognize. I pretended not to notice and started walking faster. It was still there, barely moving, but still coming in my direction. My heart began to beat faster as I started to jog down the dirt road. Then, before I knew it, I was sprinting as hard as I could away from my pursuer.

As I came to the house only minutes later, I looked back behind me, still panting. There was nothing. Again. What was going on here? I opened the front door as quickly as I could and slammed it back shut after walking in. I took a deep breath, and then another. I looked around and realized the house looked different. Everything was out of place. Things were strewn across the floor, kitchen cabinets were open with pans hanging out, and the television was sitting on the floor with the screen cracked. It was as if someone had gone through everything in our house carelessly looking for something. What could they have been looking for, I wondered. Thinking of the journal, I ran upstairs to check on it.

    I ran up the stairs as quickly as I could, hoping that whoever had been here was long gone and wouldn't jump out at me. Fear overcame me as I entered my room and looked toward the desk where I had last left the journal. As I approached, I saw that it was gone. I checked under the desk and on my bed. Still no luck. Why would someone go through this much trouble just for the journal? I sat down in my chair to recollect my thoughts. What was next? What should I do now? How had someone found out about the journal? I had no idea. What could I do? My family was gone, the journal was gone, someone or something had been following me around today, and the house had been ransacked.

I turned to my computer, which was thankfully still in one piece, and started typing. I had to find out more about this cult, The Blood of the Earth. What was their connection to all of this, if any? Almost nothing came up in the search. Of the few articles that came up only one stood out. It was titled, "The Blood of the Earth: Are They Real or Only a Rumor?" When I clicked on the link it took me to a local newspaper website which I recognized from one of my previous searches. The article had been published in 1982. There was a large image of a burnt corpse at the top of the page. The caption read, "A local woman whose murder was never solved by police, possibly a victim of the cult The Blood of the Earth."

I read on, "The Blood of the Earth has been talked down by authorities as only a rumor, but the large amount of unexplained deaths in the area over the past four years may prove otherwise. Rumors of the cult have been circulating since before the turn of the century, but no evidence has ever been found to prove their existence. Neither have there been any confirmed members of the group in this time. There have been a number of unexplained disappearances in this time, most notably in the old Riley home, that have remained unsolved. These have increased almost twice as much in the past four years and have also come to include unsolved murders, which the police only investigated for a number of weeks before giving up. Many locals have begun pointing fingers at The Blood of the Earth, but not one of them knows who exactly to point to. Are they real or just a rumor? We may never know."

    I tried searching for more articles, but it seemed as if this had been the only one. Why was there so little information on a cult that has been rumored to be in existence for over a century? I sighed and shut down the computer. My knee crashed into the desk when I heard the door slam shut downstairs. Someone else was here. Bolting up from my chair, I ran silently to the door and opened it slowly. I peaked my head out from behind the door and scanned the hallway. It was empty.

I took a deep breath and continued into the hallway with my hands still shaking. When I came to the top of the stairs, I stopped. Waiting, and listening for footsteps, I heard none. Just as I picked up my foot to move forward, I heard something fall and shatter on the floor. It had come from the kitchen. I could hear my heart pounding in my chest as I snuck down the first step and then the second. I couldn't see anything from here, but I knew that someone or something was here with me. As I jumped from the last step to the floor, I looked into the kitchen slowly. I wanted to run, run away from this terrible house and leave this nightmare behind me, but I knew I couldn't. I sighed with relief when I saw nothing in the kitchen. There was a shattered glass cup on the floor but nothing was moving. As I stepped forward into the kitchen I saw it. It wasn't a person, it was some…thing.

CHAPTER 11
July 26, 2000

I felt as if my heart was about to burst from my chest, it was beating so hard. The thing that stood before me had the same basic shape of a person but much more horrifying. Its eyes were as black as death, and it had claw-like fingers. The mouth was larger than it should have been and looked out of proportion to the rest of its face. Its head was bald and instead had two huge horns coming out of it. The strangest thing was that it was wearing ordinary clothes. It was wearing khakis with a blue button up shirt, as if it were a normal human being. We just stood there and stared for a moment, waiting for the other to move. I found that I couldn't. It was as if I was paralyzed with fear.

I saw it begin to move. I didn't know what it was doing. It started with one step forward and then lunged at me. It took me by surprise, I wasn't ready, and I wasn't sure what to do. It grabbed me and brought me to the floor in an instant. I couldn't fight back. It was too strong. It had me pinned to the floor. I wasn't sure what it was going to do with me, but I knew that it was nothing good.

The thing lifted one of its arms from me and formed a fist. This freed my arm and I did the first thing that I could think of. I punched it in the face. I hadn't hit it very hard, but I did startle it enough to get it to fall off of me. I jumped up from the floor and ran as hard as I could away from this thing. It didn't stay startled for very long, but it got up and ran after me after only a second. I ran into the kitchen looking around for something to use when I saw a knife sitting on the counter. I picked it up as quickly as I could and held it up to defend myself from my attacker. As soon as I turned around, it was there. It grabbed me by the shoulders and shook me. I didn't know what to do and didn't have any time to think. A moment later it was screeching in pain and lying on the floor in a pool of its own blood. There was a knife in its stomach. I looked down at my hands and saw that they too were covered in blood. I didn't remember how I had done it, but at least that thing was down.

I had to leave this house now before any more of these things, if any, came. But first, I needed something to protect myself with. I couldn't use that knife again. It was still stuck inside that…monster. It wasn't worth the risk of getting it back out either. I looked around the kitchen. I knew there had to be more of them around somewhere. I opened one of the drawers, only to find silverware. The best weapons in there were a fork and a butter knife. Moving on to the next drawer, I found several knives and other cooking instruments. I grabbed two knives out of the drawer, holding one and shoving the other into my pocket. I hoped it wouldn't cut me. Then I ran for the back door. Pulling it open, I let it slam into the wall before running into the forest.

I didn't really know where I was going, but it didn't matter as long as I was getting away from that house. I had been running for what seemed like an hour when my feet started to hurt. There was a sharp pain in them every time my foot touched the ground. I had to stop.

I sat down and examined my feet. They were covered in blood and broken glass. I had forgotten about the glass on the floor of the kitchen when I ran to get the knife. I hadn't even felt it, but I did now. My feet were shaking. I spent the next couple minutes slowly picking out each and every piece of glass from my foot and throwing them off into the woods. After each piece came out a small fountain of blood would gush out from the wound. The sight of it added to the pain I felt.

The Whispering

Once every piece of glass was out of my foot, I attempted to stand back up. Lifting my leg up, I put my foot to the ground for leverage only to feel an even sharper pain than before. I sat back down as fresh blood poured from the punctures in my foot. It was time for a break. I told myself. I couldn't go on like this, I had to rest. I took a deep breath and lay down on the blood-stained grass. Closing my eyes, I dreamt of my family, wishing them back.

*****

I awoke with a start. I had heard something. A voice. Looking around, I noticed that it was dark. The voice came again in a hushed whisper. Then I remembered, it was the whispers. They were back, unfortunately, for another torturous night. As if it wasn't bad enough already, the one voice was joined by a number of other voices in my head. I tried to listen to them to understand what they were saying. They seemed clearer tonight than they had before. I felt that I could almost understand them.

"You can't," was all I could make out of one whisper.

"How did you?" another started before it was silenced by another.

"Why did I have to?" asked another.

This was the most I had ever understood from them. I lay there listening to the whispers all night, only interrupted by sleep for a few moments. Before being awoken again and again by the horrible voices, I wished they would go away. I wished that things would just be normal again.

CHAPTER 12
July 27, 2000

After several hours of sleepless agony, I watched as the sun finally rose into the sky once again. Slowly the whispers one by one stopped speaking until I was finally left in peace. I lifted up one of my feet, checking to see if it was in any better condition than the day before. It wasn't. It was covered in dried blood and was throbbing with pain. What could I do? I couldn't just lie there forever, but I could barely move with my feet in the condition they were in. At least I was safe, for the moment. I knew that the thing in the house wasn't dead, but hopefully it was too badly hurt to come after me. I didn't hear anything around me either. The only sounds around me were the rustling of the leaves above, the distant flow of the stream, and the birds chirping and singing. I much preferred these to last night's whispers.

I closed my eyes, hoping to be able to finally get some sleep. My eyes had been begging for the chance to shut for the past week, but the whispers had prevented me from getting any real sleep since they had first started. I had just begun to slip into unconsciousness when I heard a snap.

My eyes shot open. I grabbed my knife which now lay beside my head and sat up. I examined the woods surrounding me tree by tree, trying to find the source of the sound. There was nothing that I could see. Then, from behind a tree, I saw something dark jump out, running quickly. It was only a squirrel. It jumped up onto another tree and climbed up. That was a relief. For a moment I had thought that maybe the monster from the house had followed me here.

I was lying back down when I saw a shadow cover my body. Looking up, I saw it. The monster was here. I didn't understand. How had it recovered so quickly? It was reaching down for my head when I held up the knife and stabbed it in the foot. I dug it in as deeply as I could and left it there, buried in its flesh. The thing yelled out in pain. I rolled over onto my stomach to avoid its other foot coming down on me. Reaching down into my pocket, I accidentally cut my finger a bit as I pulled out the spare knife, leaving smeared blood on my pants. I rolled again, trying to get back up to face my attacker. I pulled myself up against a tree as the creature ran for me once again. It ran straight into the knife blade which I had held up in my defense. I closed my eyes as blood sprayed all over my face. I spat out the little bit of blood that had entered my mouth quickly. It tasted horrible, like poison.

The monster had stopped moving. I looked down at my hand which still clutched the knife, and I saw it was lodged into the monster's skull right above the eye. It was dead, and my body was drenched with its blood. This was a relief. Now I had one less thing to worry about. I took a deep breath and wondered what I was supposed to do next. First, I had to get something to bandage my legs, I decided. I spent the next few minutes ripping off the monster's shirt, tearing it into pieces, and covering my feet with it. I used what was left of the shirt to get as much of the thing's blood off of my body as I could.

Using the tree as support, I stood up. The pain that engulfed my feet was almost unbearable, but I knew I had to. I reached down and pulled my knives back out of the monster, wiping the blood on the grass. Now what?

I leaned back against the tree, wondering what I could do and where I could go. Where was my family? They had to be somewhere. I knew that they hadn't actually just vanished. I knew I couldn't get very far with my feet in this condition. Maybe we had some sort of medicine at the house, I wondered. That would be my best bet. Now that this monster was dead it should be safe to go back, right? I wasn't completely sure, but I had to risk it.

I pushed myself away from the tree and took a step forward. I winced as my foot touched the ground and I put my weight on it. I took a breath and took another step forward. It wasn't safe to stay out here in the woods anymore, and I had to keep on moving. As painful as it was, I continued on at a slow pace back towards the house.

CHAPTER 13
July 27, 2000

Opening the door, I peered into the house looking for any more of those things that had attacked me earlier. It seemed empty to me. I took one painful step inside. The makeshift bandage I made was now completely covered in blood to the point that it was now dripping. I had started leaving a trail of blood about half way back to the house. I sorely hoped that nothing would use it to find me, but I knew I would probably only have a limited amount of time here before something else came. After double checking the house for any intruders, I went upstairs in search of the medicine cabinet. I had an idea of where it might be, but didn't know its exact location in the house since we had just moved in.

It didn't take long for me to find it in a cabinet in our bathroom. I pulled it out and examined everything, looking for anything that might help. The only thing that I found was some disinfectant medicine that also relieved pain. It was better than nothing. I sat down on the toilet and gently unwrapped the bandages from my feet. My nose crinkled at the smell. I had to look away for a moment, they were covered in a mixture of dried and fresh blood, and the cuts were deep.

The cuts were filled with dirt along with the blood, so I decided it would be best to take a shower before applying the medicine. Trying to ignore the pain I felt in my feet, I ran into my room to grab fresh clothes and a towel. I quickly turned the water on and stepped into the shower. The water made my feet sting more than before, but I watched as dirt and blood washed away from them. It only took a couple minutes before I couldn't bear it anymore and cut the water off, grabbing up the towel and drying off quickly.

I sat back down on the toilet, pulled the top of the medicine and began rubbing the lotion inside onto the cuts. It stung, but it wasn't as bad as the pain I had felt in the shower only moments ago. After I had used the entire bottle and my feet were coated with the slimy lotion, I looked around for something else to use as a bandage. There was nothing of any real use, so I sighed and settled on using an entire roll of toilet paper.

Five minutes later, I emerged from the bathroom feeling much better than before, and also looking much cleaner. My feet didn't sting quite as badly now. I walked back downstairs and sat on the couch so that I could form a plan. What could I possibly do that could help the situation? Everything was so confusing. I knew that I couldn't stay here any longer. It wasn't safe anymore since that monster had broken in. Maybe if I went into town, I could find Uncle Ray. He might know what to do. He might even know something about The Blood of the Earth cult. I wasn't exactly sure, but I thought that maybe that cult had something to do with my families' disappearance. They had to, because there was no one else to suspect.

It was settled. I would go to town in search of Uncle Ray and see if he has any information on The Blood of the Earth and their connections to all of this. I went back into the kitchen to stock back up on knives before leaving the house. I grabbed two knives and added them to the ones I already had in my pocket. That should be enough, I told myself.

The walk down the drive way wasn't as creepy this time around. After killing the monster in the woods, I felt like I would probably be able to do it again if I had to. The thing I had seen in the distance last time had probably been that creature anyway, so I should be safe enough this time around. Once I came up to the main road, I could see that it had a lot more traffic today than yesterday. It seemed to be backed up but only on one side. The traffic coming out of town seemed to be nonexistent.

There must've been a wreck up ahead, closer to town. I kept on walking until I came to the problem. There *had* been a wreck. There were two cars flipped over in the ditch with a big van truck swerved into both lanes of traffic. The road here was completely surrounded by red and blue flashing lights and police sirens. Where were the medics and ambulances? It was strange because I seemed to recognize one of the wrecked cars sitting in the ditch. Then it hit me, and I ran toward it praying that I would be wrong. In the drivers' side of a flipped pick-up truck sat my unconscious uncle with blood running down his face.

CHAPTER 14
July 27, 2000

I stood there staring in disbelief. First my family and now my uncle? How had this happened? At first, I wasn't sure if he was still alive, but then I saw his chest rise slowly and then fall back down. He was still breathing. I looked around urgently. Where was the ambulance? Why weren't they helping him? I had to get them to help him. I ran up to one of the police officers who seemed like he was in charge. He looked startled when I came up to him.

"Sir," I tried to sound respectful, "There's an injured man in that truck down there in that ditch. Why is no one helping him?"

"Now son," he answered slowly, "I need you to calm down a bit, now. We're working on it. Now if you would just leave the area, we can do our job."

"You need to go down and help him," my voice came out louder than I had meant, "Now!"

The police officer looked frustrated, but took a deep breath before answering, "We can't do anything for that man. He's dead."

That couldn't have been right, I had seen Uncle Ray breathing, and he *was* still alive. Why would this man lie to me? "No," I answered hesitantly, "No, he isn't dead. I just saw him. He was breathing!"

"Okay son, just calm down," the officer answered. He took me by the shoulder with a firm grip as he signaled someone behind me.

"What are you doing!" I exclaimed. I tried looking to see who he had signaled to, but the officer's grip was too strong. It was no use trying to break free from him.

Two bulky police officers jogged up to us. The man holding me pushed me from his grip over to them as they took me by the shoulders with one on each side. We began walking forward toward the town and away from the crash. I couldn't move the upper half of my body. They were too strong. My yelling didn't help either. They would only tighten their grip every time I did. We just kept walking until we had passed all of the police cars. They threw me down to the ground and stood there behind me. I knew they weren't going to let me go back to the wreck, so I just looked back one last time and continued on to town.

I wandered through the main street while pondering what to do. Sitting down on the first bench outside the bookstore, I went back through what had happened today. My mind was jumbled, and I couldn't quite remember the order of events. I tried to remember how I had gotten here. Then I recalled Uncle Ray and his bloodied body sitting in the over-turned truck. How had I just left him there? I had to do something. Then I saw an ambulance speeding down the road in my direction with its siren wailing in my ears. That was strange. I knew there hadn't been an ambulance at the wreck when I had been there. I hadn't seen one pass by on the way here. Then I thought, "What if they had figured out that Uncle Ray *was* still alive, and they were taking him to the hospital now?" I had to follow it and find out.

I got back up on my feet and ran after it. It wasn't long before it was so far ahead of me that I could no longer see it, but I knew where the hospital was. My feet began to burn once again. The medicine was wearing off, but I knew I couldn't stop. I had to see if they had Uncle Ray. He was the only family I had left out here.

Trying to catch my breath, I was standing outside of the hospital five minutes later. The hospital was probably the biggest building in the town although it was pretty small compared to other hospitals I had seen in bigger cities. I didn't know where the ambulance entrance was, and I doubted that they would let me in anyway. I reached for the door handle when I suddenly got an uneasy feeling. I didn't understand it, but I turned around and saw a dark figure standing in the middle of the street staring at me.

It didn't take long for me to recognize it. It had horns on its head and claws for fingers. How had it survived? Then, I saw its eyes. They weren't black like the last time, but they were red. Red as blood. I also noticed that this one seemed to be wearing a business suit rather than casual clothes as the last one had. How many of these were there? The thing took a step forward in my direction and then another. It was coming for me.

I quickly swung the door wide open and ran into the building, hoping that the mass of people here would scare it away. Then I realized there was no mass of people. The hospital interior was practically empty besides a young blonde woman sitting at the desk in front of me. She looked puzzled by my being here. I tried to look calm as I walked over to her. I forced a smile.

"Hi," I began, knowing there wasn't much time, "I was wondering where I might find my uncle. I think he was just brought in by the ambulance."

The woman still looked confused, "Um...I wouldn't know anything about that. The ambulance comes in on the other side of the hospital near the ER," she turned and pointed down the hall, "You can get there if you just go that way."

"Okay, thanks," I said quickly as I started walking down the hall. I knew that the monster could walk in at any second. I hoped that the woman would have enough sense to lock herself in somewhere once it came in.

I had been walking for a couple of minutes when I realized two things. First, I hadn't heard any screams behind me that indicated the monster walking in, and second, I hadn't seen a single person here since the woman at the desk. As I continued walking, I wondered why a hospital this large would be so empty. I rounded corner after corner only to see another sign for the ER. How big was this place anyway? After about another minute, I came to a large room occupied by only one other person and a sign indicating that this was the ER. The other person was another receptionist, but this time she was a red head. I groaned as I walked over to her.

She smiled as I approached, "Hi, how can I help you?"

I forced another smile in return, "Yes, I am looking for the man they brought in from the ambulance. He's my uncle."

The woman looked baffled, "Man? No, the person they brought in from the ambulance was a woman."

CHAPTER 15
July 27, 2000

"What?" I was confused. "No, my Uncle should be here."

"All that I know," the woman explained, "is that the ambulance only brought in one patient, and it was a woman. So unless she is related to you as well, I suggest you leave."

I stood there bewildered at this turn of events. Was I honestly surprised? The police officer had told me that he was dead even though we both knew he wasn't. Had they really just left him there to die? Why would they? What was their motive? Then I thought that maybe The Blood of the Earth had something to do with all of this. Maybe they had set the whole thing up. What if they were more than just a rumor and they had kidnapped my family and murdered my uncle? All of these thoughts continued to flow in my head, but the question I kept on coming to was, "Why?" Why was any of this happening?

I realized I was still standing in front of the red headed woman. She seemed angry, "I told you to leave. Did you hear me?"

"Oh," I tried to think of an explanation but only backed away without saying another word. I had to get back to the wreck to find Uncle Ray. Hopefully the police would be gone by now. They hadn't seemed overly concerned with him, so he would probably still be there. At least I hoped he would.

    I turned around, seeing an exit, and ran out of the building. Then I remembered that thing was still out here, somewhere. I scanned the area looking slowly from a bakery to my left over to a school on my right. There was nothing, at least nothing that I could see from here. I would just have to be careful and keep a look out for it. I began walking down the main road back towards the wreck. It only took a few minutes before I realized I had gone too far. There had been nothing there, and I had accidentally passed it. I turned back around looking at the area where a major wreck had been only an hour ago. Where had they taken my uncle other than the hospital?

At that moment, something lunged at me from the woods bringing me to the ground. I jumped back to my feet to see the red-eyed monster standing in front of me. Reaching into my pocket, I pulled out two knives, one for each hand. I noticed that none of the cars seemed to notice the monster on the side of the road. The red-eyed monster jumped at me with its claws outstretched towards my face. I deflected its attack with the swipe of a blade, cutting the tips off of its claws. I thrust the other knife towards its chest just missing as it stepped back.

I advanced towards it, holding both knives in front of my body protectively. It took a step back before charging towards me once again but this time with its teeth barred. I stepped to the side as quickly as I could bringing both knives down on it as it passed by. Blood splattered in the air as the knives cut two deep holes into its back. It screeched out in pain. Pulling the knives out, I thrust them back into the monster, but this time I was aiming for its neck. This brought the creature to the ground as a massive stream of blood fell from the fresh wound. I pulled the knives back out once again and examined them. They were completely drenched in dark red blood.

    The monster let out screams of agony as I stood over it staring at its blood. I looked down at its face, and I saw the hatred it had for me. It looked as if it wanted to kill me even more than it had already tried. Its screaming was too much for me to bear; the sound seemed to pierce through my ears. I had to end it. I brought the blades back down on the monster, but this time buried them in its chest. It let out one last painful scream before there was finally silence.

I stood back up over its lifeless corpse and watched it for a moment before bending back over to clean the blades on the grass. I guessed that I was once again covered in blood. I stood up, taking a deep breath, wondering how things had gotten this bad. That was when I saw it. A car was speeding down the road when it started pulling to the right side of the asphalt. It was coming right for me.

CHAPTER 16
July 27, 2000

I jumped from where I had been standing as quickly as I could and landed on top of a bush several feet away. The car came crashing down before my eyes, crushing the monster's corpse with it. One of the tires flew from the car in my direction. I barely had enough time to duck down in order to dodge it. The car didn't explode on impact as they did in movies, but instead shattered into several pieces which flew up into the air. Only the main body of the car was left intact.

Looking into the drivers' side of the vehicle, I noticed that it had not been a person driving the car. Rather it had been another creature which had been following me that was sitting in the driver's seat. This hadn't been an accident. The thing had been trying to kill me. Its head was resting on the wheel of the car covered in blood. It seemed to be unconscious, at least for now.

I got back up and walked over to it examining the wreckage. The car was completely totaled. It was an older sports car. No wonder the airbags hadn't come out. I looked down on the bloody creature in the driver's side. It was still breathing, slowly, but not for long I was sure. I pulled a knife back out and slit its throat. This was half out of pity and half just as a precaution. How many of these creatures were there out there, I wondered, and why did they all want to kill me? I slipped the knife back into my back pocket and decided to go back to town and search for Uncle Ray.

*****

Back in town, I thought that I should check the hospital again. They could have been lying when they said that the person brought was a woman. As I walked down the main road back toward the hospital, I felt uneasy. The town seemed to be emptier than before to the point of almost being deserted. There was absolutely no one in the streets. I could just barely make out one or two store clerks in their buildings, but they were lacking customers. Where had everyone gone?

As I stepped across the main road over to the sidewalk across from the hospital, I caught sight of someone. It wasn't just someone, but it was a small child. He was standing on the sidewalk across the street directly in front of the hospital entrance, and he was staring at me. It felt strange. It was as if he wasn't looking at me physically, but he was seeing every part of me. It was like he could read my thoughts, emotions, and soul. A chill ran down my spine as his gaze continued. I couldn't move. My heart stopped when I realized that this was my brother, Josh. Well, at least he looked like Josh. This one had eyes similar to the monsters, but his eyes were glowing blue instead of black or red.

I was startled once again when the kid disappeared as I blinked. Maybe it hadn't been real, I told myself, and maybe it was just wishful thinking. I did miss my family tremendously, after all. Taking a deep breath, I stepped across the street and walked into the hospital entrance. Expecting to see the blonde receptionist again, I was instead greeted by no one. The hospital interior was completely deserted. Had everyone fled the town? Regardless of who was or wasn't here, I was going to find Uncle Ray, and I was going to start here. The receptionist may have been lying before when she had said that the patient brought in was a woman. I had to check for myself. It was worth a shot anyway.

The walk to the ER seemed shorter this time around, and upon arrival, I was once again greeted by no one. The red-headed receptionist was gone as well, thankfully. The door to the ER hospital rooms was, conveniently, open. I walked over and swung it out completely, checking for anyone in the hallway. It seemed clear enough. I stepped in and began walking down the dull, white hallway, checking inside each room. The majority of these were empty besides the beds and counters full of assorted drugs and medicines.

Finally, at the end of the hall, I came to a room with a patient. They were lying down in the bed wearing a full body cast that covered even the head aside from the eyes and nose. The eyes were closed and I could tell that they belonged to a man. Walking closer, I caught sight of a clipboard on the counter. I picked it up and looked at the name, "Raymond Riley." Why had the receptionist lied before? It was as if no one in town wanted me to speak to Uncle Ray today.

I jumped when I heard heavy footsteps coming towards the room. Someone was here. I had to hide. If they hadn't wanted me here before, then they wouldn't want me here now. Looking around the room, there weren't many options. As the footsteps got closer and closer, my heartbeat raced faster. I finally threw open a cabinet door under the drug counter and climbed in. It was tight, but it was all I had. I quickly pulled the cabinet door shut as I caught a glimpse of a figure when it appeared in the doorway. It was dressed as a doctor but had horns, claws, and pitch-black eyes.

CHAPTER 17
July 27, 2000

It hadn't seen me, I told myself. It couldn't have. Why was it here? What was it doing with my uncle? I realized that I was breathing heavier than normal. Raising my hand to my face, I cupped it over my mouth to prevent any unwanted sounds from escaping. I could feel my heart pounding in my chest. What could I do? Nothing, not while I was in this cabinet. I knew that I had to kill that thing before it did anything to Uncle Ray. I took a deep breath, ready to step out wielding my knives in both hands.

There was a loud thump as if something had been thrown against the wall. My hand reached for the cabinet door. I swung it open and peered back into the room. My uncle was held up against the wall by the creature with his cast covered in blood where the claws had dug into his flesh. His eyes were staring at me, pleading for help. Standing up, I pulled the knives from my pockets. Holding one in each hand, I charged at the creature. It hadn't noticed my presence, I assumed it was too occupied with killing my uncle to worry about anything else. The knife blades quickly found their way into its lower back, and it let out a scream of both surprise and pain.

I was thrown to the wall opposite my Uncle as the creatures arms flung around searching for the source of its agony. Pain shot through my entire body as my back collided with the counter. Falling down to the floor, I couldn't move. The knives were still buried in the creatures back, dripping with blood. I could see my uncle fall to the floor on the other side of the room as the creature turned its attention to me. The floor shook as it slowly stepped towards me. It wasn't long before it was standing over me with its claws raised to strike. I closed my eyes, and waited for it to happen. I was waiting for my death.

Death never came, and I heard the sound of the creature's whimpers from farther away. I opened my eyes and saw that the creature was no longer standing over me, but instead there was only a puddle of blood. The blood was smeared into the hallway as if something had dragged it out there. Whatever it was, I didn't want to anger that. I slowly stood back up, checking my back for blood. It had only been bruised, but it hurt enough for me not to forget that it was there. I stepped towards my uncle who was on the floor, also covered in blood. The blood. There had been so much of it these past two days.

    Kneeling down beside my uncle, I checked to see if he was okay. His eyes were closed once again. I held my hand up against his nose and mouth checking to see if he was breathing. I waited for what seemed like an hour, but he never did exhale. I sighed. My uncle was dead now. He had been my only hope of finding my parents. Then I remembered the kid I had seen, the one who had looked like Josh. Maybe it had been Josh. Maybe he was out there somewhere, but what about his eyes? Why had they been glowing blue? Maybe I had imagined all of it. I wanted to believe that he could be out there somewhere waiting for me to find him and my parents.

    I stood back up, deciding to search around the town for Josh. It could've been a lost cause, but I didn't care. I had to do *something*. Following the trail of smeared blood, I came into the hallway where the monster's corpse lay sprawled across the floor. Its head had been flattened. Whatever had killed it was gone now. Aside from the corpse, the hallway was as empty as it had been before. I cautiously stepped around it, heading for the exit and stopping only to retrieve the two knives still lodged in its lower back. I didn't bother to clean off the blades before stuffing them into my pockets as I continued through the hallway and out into the lobby. I turned to the exit and opened the door only to stop there in my tracks. Outside was what looked to be the entire police force. After a more careful look, I realized that these police officers weren't human. They were the same creatures that had been after me since the disappearance, and they were all pointing guns at me.

CHAPTER 18
July 27, 2000

I jumped back into the building and slammed the door shut just barely missing a round of bullets which pierced every window in sight. What was going on? Where did these things come from, and where were the actual police? The floor was littered with glass. I would have to be careful to avoid cutting my feet a second time. I turned to look for a way out. Surely the other entrance would be blocked as well, but it was at least worth a try. I sprinted through the next hallway, towards the entrance I had originally come through. The halls seemed darker than they had been before. I realized that the power must be out because there wasn't a single light on in the entire building it seemed.

It didn't take long for me to reach the entrance. I had to stop to catch my breath for a moment before walking to the door. I prayed a quick prayer before reaching for the door and opening it. To my surprise, the street was empty. Why had they barricaded the other entrance and not this one? I didn't dwell on this question for long, but instead I ran across the street and into town.

The town was completely empty now and entirely silent. I glanced back, checking for any pursuers. What I saw was the police force of monsters coming around the hospital, heading in my direction. It didn't seem like they had seen me yet, so I quickly scrambled into an alley and kneeled to the ground in order to give my legs a rest. I wondered why they were coming for me. Maybe these creatures were a part of The Blood of the Earth and wanted me gone just like the rest of my family. I couldn't let them take me. I decided that I had to get out of town.

I stood back up looking around, planning my next move. I couldn't let any of them see me as I left because as far as they knew, I was still inside the hospital. I saw a path of alleys that led to the edge of the town and eventually the forest. I was ready. Taking a deep breath, I sprinted across the street, hoping they hadn't seen me cross and continued going through alley after alley. It wasn't long before I came to a large patch of grass which separated the forest from the town. I glanced behind me quickly before entering the forest, to make sure none of them had seen me. To my despair, I saw the entire police force marching through the first alley behind me. My heart raced, and I took off into the woods.

    I didn't know where I was going, but I didn't care as long as I was getting away. It was much darker now under the cover of the leaf-filled trees. This made seeing where I was headed much harder. I had barely missed hitting more than a few tree trunks because I had been running so hard. Risking a peek behind me, I saw two creatures clad in police uniforms in close pursuit. I tried to run harder but found that I had very little energy left. It seemed as if my supply of adrenaline was dwindling down to nothingness.

I reached into my pockets and pulled the knives out, ready to defend myself if needed. I knew I couldn't stop running, but my legs ached and my feet were burning. I couldn't keep it up for much longer. My breathing was harsh and quick. I had to stop. No, I told my feet. If I wanted to live I couldn't stop. My feet didn't stop but slowly began to drag closer to the ground until catching onto a root, bringing me to the ground.

My body cried in pain both from the hard fall and the aches from running so hard for so long. I wasn't in good enough shape to do that sort of running, which I realized too late.

The two creatures came up to me and began to circle around me as if trying to decide who would attack first. I noticed that they were carrying guns as well. I looked around for my knives seeing that they were no longer in my hands. One was sitting in front of me, and the other was lodged in the ground behind me. I grabbed them both and waited for the creatures to attack. The creatures seemed to come to a decision as one of them held a gun to my head. It was too far away for me to swipe at with my knife which wouldn't have done much good for me anyway. I held one knife up, trying to decide whether I was a good enough shot to throw it at the creature. On a normal day, I knew I couldn't, but this wasn't a normal day. I didn't have any other options.

Closing my eyes, I threw the knife forward expecting a bullet to hit me at any moment. All I heard was the sound of the creature screeching as my blade slid into its head. I turned to the other creature. Its gun was held up to me now as well. I threw the other knife at it as fast as I could, catching it in its shoulder. The gun went off hitting a tree behind me. I smiled as hope returned to me.

The smile faded as over a dozen more monsters dressed as police men walked up towards me. To my surprise, they were led by a human. It took me a moment to recognize him as Uncle Ray.

CHAPTER 19
July 27, 2000

How was this possible? I had seen my uncle just a moment ago, dead on the floor wearing a full body cast. He laughed as he saw my confusion. This was not the uncle I had remembered. This one seemed almost evil. The horde of creatures formed a line behind my uncle.

"I bet you're confused right now, aren't you?" he asked with an evil looking smile on his face. I only stared at him, unable to find words to answer with.

"Well, maybe I can help with that, before we finish you," he was still smiling. It was creepy at this point, "You've heard of The Blood of the Earth by now, I imagine?" I answered only with a slow nod.

"Then you know why we have to do this terrible act every ten years?"

"What?" I answered, "No, there's no reason for anyone to kidnap people."

Uncle Ray sighed, "So, you don't understand. Well, where can I begin? I know you found the journal that we placed in your yard. Don't worry. It *was* real. It details the first time The Blood of the Earth was ever called to act. You see, the Riley family had the old graveyard that used to be behind that house of yours torn down. That had been the resting place of many ancestors belonging to the founders of The Blood of the Earth. It had been a terrible crime done to them, robbing them of their deceased loved ones. Their souls cried out for justice, and the founders acted for them. At first they warned the Riley family, they told them to get out of the house. They didn't listen, so more desperate measures were called for."

"The founders kidnapped the family, sparing the child and made their justice. Their bodies were added to the collection still buried where the graveyard had originally been. This had not been enough though, the founders realized that they couldn't be discovered, so they went back for the child and took him in with them. Raising him as their own, he became my grandfather, and your great-grandfather."

This was a shock. I didn't realize that my family had gone through so much, but why had the names not matched. My great-grandfather was named Nicholas.

"They made him change his name, but only his first name, so that if anyone found his journal, it would not be traced as easily. It was later decided, after more people moved in and out of the house, that we had to make an example of them. In 1910, your great-grandfather assisted the founders in the kidnapping and murder of the Mosley family. Afterwards, he felt so guilty, he left the founders and moved as far away as he could, starting a new life. The founders found others when needed to assist them in their tradition which took place every decade."

"I found my way back here by chance. I moved here looking for a job, but heard stories which I dismissed at first. Upon hearing that our family was involved I rushed here to see what it was about. I made my connections with people in the town and realized that it was what we were all meant to do, so in 1980, I assisted The Blood of the Earth. It gave me such a rush and sense of duty that I couldn't leave, I couldn't stop. Now here I am."

I only stared at him in disbelief and disgust. How could a man be so evil?

"Now, I bet you want to know how you and your family came into all of this. Well, after the last ritual in 1990, people started hearing more about it and saying that the house was haunted. I was worried that we wouldn't have anyone to make an example of this year, so I suggested the house to my brother. I wasn't sure if I could do it to family, but I knew it was for a good cause. I had to suck it up and do it. Now that that part of the job is done, it's about time we finished it. Soon, you will join the rest of your family."

"Wait," I exclaimed, "I don't understand. What about the creatures? And I did see my brother Josh out in the town just earlier. What about them? Can you explain them?" I was motioning towards the police creatures all around me.

My uncle looked at me, obviously puzzled, and then smiled. "Yes, this happens a lot actually. Everyone reacts differently to it. The ones who find the journal and go down to the original gravesites are the ones overwhelmed with fear, and something happens which causes them to go insane. I would guess that has something to do with the spirits of those graves which were disturbed a century ago. They still linger down there, even now."

"You're crazy!" I yelled.

"No," he laughed, "Actually, that would be you. You see, all of these people standing around me are cops. They've been after you all day, especially after they found that corpse on the side of the road. You were walking around the town covered in blood after all. As for your brother, I don't know, you're the crazy one here."

"Wait," I said, "But, you were there in the hospital, one of them attacked you."

"I was never in the hospital," he answered matter-of-factly; "You imagined it, along with everything else. The only thing that seems to happen to all of you is the whispering you seem to hear. I would guess that would be the spirits speaking to you and each other."

"They can't be spirits!" I yelled, "This can't be real. If anything, they'd have to be demons."

"Yes, maybe," he said. "Especially after all the people you've killed in the past couple days, I wouldn't be surprised. Oh well, now is time for these police officers to finish my job for me."

One of the police officers began to walk towards me. I saw that he wasn't a monster anymore, but a dark-haired man. How could this be? Maybe all of this had been a dream. Maybe I would wake up in a moment, and see my family again. The police officer stood behind me, putting his hands to my neck. My heart raced. I held my hands up to pull him away from me.

The last thing I remember is a sharp pain in my neck and then pure light. I saw my family again in the distance and rushed toward them. They were smiling.

Continue on for a preview of the next chapter in Jana Harper's dark suspense series
The Whispering Earth
Book 2: Shadow Cult

CHAPTER 1
April 3, 1980

The glare of the sun blinded me as I reached for my sunglasses, making sure not to let go of the wheel as I did so. I knew I had taken a wrong turn at the last intersection. The road was much too busy to attempt a three-point-turn, and there hadn't been any roads for me to turn around on yet. The sun's glare didn't help me much either.

The road suddenly became much easier to see as I slipped the sunglasses onto my face. There was a red sports car in front of me going ten miles below the speed limit. The driver obviously didn't know how to drive that car. I tried honking my horn, but the driver paid no attention to my frustration. I glanced at the other side of the road to see that there wasn't any oncoming traffic, and then I pulled my car to that side. My foot jerked down on the gas pedal as soon as I was clear of the red sports car. I waited for my car to speed ahead, but after a moment, I noticed that we were right next to each other. The man in the car next to mine shot me a dirty look as he slowly sped ahead of me.

My frustration quickly transformed into fury as I pushed down on the gas pedal even more. I couldn't just let this jerk get away with this! I honked my horn once again as my car gradually caught up with the sports car. We were now both going well over the speed limit. The other driver glanced over at me with a grin on his face. What was wrong with this guy? I pushed down on the gas once more as I glared at the other driver. I watched as his grin changed into a look of horror. He was looking down the road ahead.

My heart stopped when I looked back at the road. A large van-truck honked its horn at me. We were about fifty feet away from a head-on collision. The man in the sports car must have hit his brakes because he was several feet behind my car. My heart pounded in my chest as I grabbed the wheel and jerked it to the side. Miraculously, I made it back into the correct lane just before colliding with the front-end of the truck. I heard one last honk from the truck before it rounded a corner and was out of sight. I took a deep breath and sighed. That was close.

After a moment of peaceful driving, I saw an old dirt road to my right. I put on my turning signal before mashing the brakes slightly and pulling in. There was no end to the dirt road in sight. I noticed an old mailbox to my right. I realized that the dirt road must be a driveway for an old house. This got me interested, so I decided to drive down the road a bit further rather than turn around here.

I had been driving for a minute or so before I caught a glimpse of the house. It seemed dark because it blocked most of the sun from my view. What little sunlight that hit my eyes blinded me to the details of the house. I continued driving.

As I got closer, it became easier to see the smaller details of the house. It was an older house with three floors. The dark grey paint on its outside walls was still wet. Overall, the house didn't look like the typical 'old abandoned house in the woods,' but at the same time it didn't quite look like it was being lived in either.

My car came to a stop once I realized that I had come to the end of the driveway. I knew I should turn around here. There was no reason for me to stay for any amount of time, but I felt drawn to the place. Logic was overpowered by curiosity as I felt my hands put the car into park and then pull the keys from the ignition. Forgetting the juvenile saying about cats and their curiosity, I opened my car door and stepped out. The air was warmer out here, yet I still felt a chill run down my back. I knew that I shouldn't be doing this, but I couldn't get myself to stop.

I walked up the three steps that led up to the front porch and reached for the doorknob. My hand stopped just inches away. Should I knock first? It didn't look like anyone was living here, but it felt wrong not to. I balled my fist and knocked on the black wooden door. I held my breath as I waited for an answer. I knocked a second time as I continued to wait with anticipation. After a minute, there was no answer. I exhaled and took a deep breath. My original presumption still held up; it seemed that no one was living here at the moment. I reached out for the doorknob once again. My palms started to sweat as I gripped the doorknob and began to twist it. It only turned slightly before stopping. It was locked.

What had I been thinking? Of course it was locked. Why wouldn't it be? I almost felt disappointed as I walked back to my car. I had barely reached the door of the car when I heard a strange chanting sound. It was strange because it sounded as if it were coming from behind the house. This got me interested. I cast out logic once again as I stepped in the direction of the chanting. The sound of it got louder with every step that I took. I could now hear each individual voice, but I didn't understand what they were saying. It sounded as if there were about five or six of them chanting in some other language.

I reached the end of the house and decided to hide behind the corner for fear that they might catch sight of me. I breathed deeply before sneaking a glance toward them. There were five of them standing in a circle all dressed in black robes. They were all men and were standing around a fire. I wondered if they were performing some sort of ritual.

To my surprise, the chanting stopped suddenly. I glanced back at them to see what was wrong. My heart stopped for a moment when I saw five pairs of eyes looking back at me. Without a second thought I ran back to my car and got in. I quickly jammed the key into the ignition and put the car in reverse. I backed out at an angle so that I could put the car back into drive and quickly drove back to the main road.

I didn't look back into the rearview mirror until I reached the road. There were no pursuers as far as I could tell. I looked back at the road. Had I come from the left or the right? I couldn't remember, so I took a right and hoped that I was going the right way.

Continue on for a preview of Jana Harper's new sci-fi series
Screaming Stars
Book 1: Shot Into Screaming Stars

CHAPTER 1

I woke to the sound of screaming. My eyes shot open at the sound of it. A piercing wail that cut through the metal walls of my room as if they weren't even there. How could this be? I was the only person aboard this ship. What could be causing such a terrible sound?

I threw off my covers and got out of the bed, searching for my clothes. I needed to go out and investigate the source of the screaming. Whatever it was, it didn't belong on this ship.

My ship.

The *Regitano* had been my home for the past five years. I hadn't allowed another human being aboard since it had first come into my possession. The only time I ever came into contact with other people was when I had to stop at refuel stations or when I stopped for supplies. You could say that I wasn't much of a people person. I much preferred the company of my robots.

For the last five years, the majority of my socializing had been with my three robot companions. My favorite thing about being alone on a ship of robots rather than humans was the lack of drama. I hated the drama that could be caused by other people. Robots didn't do that. They were purely logical and drama-free. This led to a much more stress-free life for me. It was great.

Well, it *was* great. I didn't know what was causing that screaming sound, but it was really stressing me out.

I pulled on a pair of pants and slipped on a shirt before I ran out of my room and into the control room. The screaming was much louder in this room, but I still couldn't pinpoint the source of it.

I heard the sound of metallic steps coming up behind me. Turning around, I saw that it was FR-3D, or Fred as I called him. He was walking hurriedly toward me, clearly alarmed.

"James, there seems to be a situation," Fred said as he stopped in front of me.

"Tell me about it," I replied. "That sound woke me up from a great dream I was having."

"I am sorry to hear that James," Fred said, failing to simulate an apologetic tone. "The noise is quite alarming. It does not register on my sensors as belonging to a human. My memory banks don't have any cataloged being in all of the galactic quadrants that match the specific vocal patterns of this screaming voice."

"Wait, you're telling me that this isn't a human scream?" I asked. It sounded close enough to human to me. "How can it not match anything in all of your memory banks? Are you up to date on your software?"

That had been a stupid question. Of course he was up to date on his software. I was a stickler for keeping all of my robots up to date on all of their software drivers. I *never* let them skip an update.

"Yes James, I updated just yesterday. I do not know what could be making that sound," Fred replied.

My ears were beginning to ring from the continued sound of the screaming. "One thing is for sure about this thing," I began. "It's got a great pair of lungs."

"I do believe I can pinpoint the location of the being causing the noise," Fred said helpfully.

"Yes, please do that," I said. "Then hopefully we can get it to shut up and tell us where it came from and how it got on my ship without me knowing."

Fred began walking over to the engine room, which was just to the left of the control room. We passed through the doors that separated the two rooms, and we were surrounded by the loud humming of the engines. Well, that and the ear-splitting screaming. The sound seemed to be coming from the dark corner in the far right of the engine room.

Fred led the way over to the corner and crumpled up against the wall was the most bizarre looking creature I had ever seen in my life.

"What the hell is that?" I asked incredulously.

Other Books by Jana Harper

Public School No. 4

The Whispering Earth:

The Whispering

Shadow Cult

The Cursed House

The Sacred Journal

The Final Ritual

The Silver Isles:

The Dark Priest

Jacob the Lost

Screaming Stars:

Shot Into Screaming Stars

Through the Screaming Stars

Beyond the Screaming Stars

Escape from Screaming Stars

Printed in France by Amazon
Brétigny-sur-Orge, FR